This Simiar

Clarence Day

Alpha Editions

This edition published in 2023

ISBN : 9789357949064

Design and Setting By
Alpha Editions
www.alphaedis.com
Email - info@alphaedis.com

ONE

Last Sunday, Potter took me out driving along upper Broadway, where those long rows of tall new apartment houses were built a few years ago. It was a mild afternoon and great crowds of people were out. Sunday afternoon crowds. They were not going anywhere,--they were just strolling up and down, staring at each other, and talking. There were thousands and thousands of them.

"Awful, aren't they!" said Potter.

I didn't know what he meant. When he added, "Why, these crowds," I turned and asked, "Why, what about them?" I wasn't sure whether he had an idea or a headache.

"Other creatures don't do it," he replied, with a discouraged expression. "Are any other beings ever found in such masses, but vermin? Aimless, staring, vacant-minded,--look at them! I can get no sense whatever of individual worth, or of value in men as a race, when I see them like this. It makes one almost despair of civilization."

I thought this over for awhile, to get in touch with his attitude. I myself feel differently at different times about us human-beings: sometimes I get pretty indignant when we are attacked (for there is altogether too much abuse of us by spectator philosophers) and yet at other times I too feel like a spectator, an alien: but even then I had never felt so alien or despairing as Potter. I cast about for the probable cause of our difference. "Let's remember," I said, "it's a simian civilization."

Potter was staring disgustedly at some vaudeville sign-boards.

"Yes," I said, "those for example are distinctively simian. Why should you feel disappointment at something inevitable?" And I went on to argue that it wasn't as though we were descended from eagles for instance, instead of (broadly speaking) from ape-like or monkeyish beings. Being of simian stock, we had simian traits. Our development naturally bore the marks of our origin. If we had inherited our dispositions from eagles we should have loathed vaudeville. But as cousins of the Bandarlog, we loved it. What could you expect?

Descended from eagles

TWO

If we had been made directly from clay, the way it says in the Bible, and had therefore inherited no intermediate characteristics,--if a god, or some principle of growth, had gone that way to work with us, he or it might have molded us into much more splendid forms.

But considering our simian descent, it has done very well. The only people who are disappointed in us are those who still believe that clay story. Or who--unconsciously--still let it color their thinking.

There certainly seems to be a power at work in the world, by virtue of which every living thing grows and develops. And it tends toward splendor. Seeds become trees, and weak little nations grow great. But the push or the force that is doing this, the yeast as it were, has to work in and on certain definite kinds of material. Because this yeast is in us, there may be great and undreamed of possibilities awaiting mankind; but because of our line of descent there are also queer limitations.

Strange forgotten dynasties

THREE

In those distant invisible epochs before men existed, before even the proud missing link strutted around through the woods (little realizing how we his greatgrandsons would smile wryly at him, much as our own descendants may shudder at us, ages hence) the various animals were desperately competing for power. They couldn't or didn't live as equals. Certain groups sought the headship.

Many strange forgotten dynasties rose, met defiance, and fell. In the end it was our ancestors who won, and became simian kings, and bequeathed a whole planet to us--and have never been thanked for it. No monument has been raised to the memory of those first hairy conquerors; yet had they not fought well and wisely in those far-off times, some other race would have been masters, and kept us in cages, or shot us for sport in the forests while they ruled the world.

So Potter and I, developing this train of thought, began to imagine we had lived many ages ago, and somehow or other had alighted here from some older planet. Familiar with the ways of evolution elsewhere in the universe, we naturally should have wondered what course it would take on this earth. "Even in this out-of-the-way corner of the Cosmos," we might have reflected, "and on this tiny star, it may be of interest to consider the trend of events." We should have tried to appraise the different species as they wandered around, each with its own set of good and bad characteristics. Which group, we'd have wondered, would ever contrive to rule all the rest?

And how great a development could they attain to thereafter?

FOUR

If we had landed here after the great saurians had been swept from the scene, we might first have considered the lemurs or apes. They had hands. Aesthetically viewed, the poor simians were simply grotesque; but travelers who knew other planets might have known what beauty may spring from an uncouth beginning in this magic universe.

Still--those frowzy, unlovely hordes of apes and monkeys were so completely lacking in signs of kingship; they were so flighty, too, in their ways, and had so little purpose, and so much love for absurd and idle chatter, that they would have struck us, we thought, as unlikely material. Such traits, we should have reminded ourselves, persist. They are not easily left behind, even after long stages; and they form a terrible obstacle to all high advancement.

FIVE

The bees or the ants might have seemed to us more promising. Their smallness of size was not necessarily too much of a handicap. They could have made poison their weapon for the subjugation of rivals. And in these orderly insects there was obviously a capacity for labor, and co-operative labor at that, which could carry them far. We all know that they have a marked genius: great gifts of their own. In a civilization of super-ants or bees, there would have been no problem of the hungry unemployed, no poverty, no unstable government, no riots, no strikes for short hours, no derision of eugenics, no thieves, perhaps no crime at all.

Ants are good citizens: they place group interests first.

But they carry it so far, they have few or no political rights. An ant doesn't have the vote, apparently: he just has his duties.

This quality may have something to do with their having group wars. The egotism of their individual spirits is allowed scant expression, so the egotism of the group is extremely ferocious and active. Is this one of the reasons why ants fight so much? They go in for State Socialism, yes, but they are not internationalists. And ants commit atrocities in and after their battles that are--I wish I could truly say--inhuman.

But conversely, ants are absolutely unselfish within the community. They are skilful. Ingenious. Their nests and buildings are relatively larger than man's. The scientists speak of their paved streets, vaulted halls, their hundreds of different domesticated animals, their pluck and intelligence, their individual initiative, their chaste and industrious lives. Darwin said the ant's brain was "one of the most marvelous atoms in the world, perhaps more so than the brain of man"--yes, of present-day man, who for thousands and thousands of years has had so much more chance to develop his brain.... A thoughtful observer would have weighed all these excellent qualities.

When we think of these creatures as little men (which is all wrong of course) we see they have their faults. To our eyes they seem too orderly, for instance. Repressively so. Their ways are more fixed than those of the old Egyptians, and their industry is painful to think of, it's hyper-Chinese. But we must remember this is a simian comment. The instincts of the species that you and I belong to are of an opposite kind; and that makes it hard for us to judge ants fairly.

But we and the ants are alike in one matter: the strong love of property. And instead of merely struggling with Nature for it, they also fight other ants. The custom of plunder seems to be a part of most of their wars. This has gone on for ages among them, and continues today. Raids, ferocious combats, and loot are part of an ant's regular life. Ant reformers, if there were any, might lay this to their property sense, and talk of abolishing property as a cure for the evil. But that would not help for long unless they could abolish the love of it.

Ants seem to care even more for property than we do ourselves. We men are inclined to ease up a little when we have all we need. But it is not so with ants: they can't bear to stop: they keep right on working. This means that ants do not contemplate: they heed nothing outside of their own little rounds. It is almost as though their fondness for labor had closed fast their minds.

Conceivably they might have developed inquiring minds. But this would have run against their strongest instincts. The ant is knowing and wise; but he doesn't know enough to take a vacation. The worshipper of energy is too physically energetic to see that he cannot explore certain higher fields until he is still.

Even if such a race had somehow achieved self-consciousness and reason, would they have been able therewith to rule their instincts, or to stop work long enough to examine themselves, or the universe, or to dream of any noble development? Probably not. Reason is seldom or never the ruler: it is the servant of instinct. It would therefore have told the ants that incessant toil was useful and good.

"Toil has brought you up from the ruck of things," Reason would have plausibly said. "It's by virtue of feverish toil that you have become what you are. Being endlessly industrious is the best road--for you--to the heights." And, self-reassured, they would then have had orgies of work; and thus, by devoted exertion, have blocked their advancement. Work, and order and gain would have withered their souls.

SIX

Let us take the great cats. They are free from this talent for slave-hood. Stately beasts like the lion have more independence of mind than the ants,--and a self-respect, we may note, unknown to primates. Or consider the leopards, with hearts that no tyrant could master. What fearless and resolute leopard-men they could have fathered! How magnificently such a civilization would have made its force tell!

A race of civilized beings descended from these great cats would have been rich in hermits and solitary thinkers. The recluse would not have been stigmatized as peculiar, as he is by us simians. They would not have been a credulous people, or easily religious. False prophets and swindlers would have found few dupes. And what generals they would have made! what consummate politicians!

Don't imagine them as a collection of tigers walking around on their hind-legs. They would have only been like tigers in the sense that we men are like monkeys. Their development in appearance and character would have been quite transforming.

Instead of the small flat head of the tiger, they would have had clear smooth brows; and those who were not bald would have had neatly parted hair--perhaps striped.

Their mouths would have been smaller and more sensitive: their faces most dignified. Where now they express chiefly savageness, they would have expressed fire and grace.

They would have been courteous and suave. No vulgar crowding would have occurred on the streets of their cities. No mobs. No ignominious subway-jams.

Imagine a cultivated coterie of such men and women, at a ball, dancing. How few of us humans are graceful. They would have all been Pavlovas.

Like ants and bees, the cat race is nervous. Their temperaments are high-strung. They would never have become as poised or as placid as--say--super-cows. Yet they would have had less insanity, probably, than we. Monkeys' (and elephants') minds seem precariously balanced, unstable. The great cats are saner. They are intense, they would have needed sanitariums: but fewer asylums. And their asylums would have been not for weak-minded souls, but for furies.

They would have been strong at slander. They would have been far more violent than we, in their hates, and they would have had fewer friendships.

Yet they might not have been any poorer in real friendships than we. The real friendships among men are so rare that when they occur they are famous. Friends as loyal as Damon and Pythias were, are exceptions. Good fellowship is common, but unchanging affection is not. We like those who like us, as a rule, and dislike those who don't. Most of our ties have no better footing than that; and those who have many such ties are called warm-hearted.

The super-cat-men would have rated cleanliness higher. Some of us primates have learned to keep ourselves clean, but it's no large proportion; and even the cleanest of us see no grandeur in soap-manufacturing, and we don't look to manicures and plumbers for social prestige. A feline race would have honored such occupations. J. de Courcy Tiger would have felt that nothing *but* making soap, or being a plumber, was compatible with a high social position; and the rich Vera Pantherbilt would have deigned to dine only with manicures.

None but the lowest dregs of such a race would have been lawyers spending their span of life on this mysterious earth studying the long dusty records of dead and gone quarrels. We simians naturally admire a profession full of wrangle and chatter. But that is a monkeyish way of deciding disputes, not a feline.

We fight best in armies, gregariously, where the risk is reduced; but we disapprove usually of murderers, and of almost all private combat. With the great cats, it would have been just the other way round. (Lions and leopards fight each other singly, not in bands, as do monkeys.)

As a matter of fact, few of us delight in really serious fighting. We do love to bicker; and we box and knock each other around, to exhibit our strength; but few normal simians are keen about bloodshed and killing; we do it in war only because of patriotism, revenge, duty, glory. A feline civilization would have cared nothing for duty or glory, but they would have taken a far higher pleasure in gore. If a planet of super-cat-men could look down upon ours, they would not know which to think was the most amazing: the way we tamely live, five million or so in a city, with only a few police to keep us quiet, while we commit only one or two murders a day, and hardly have a respectable number of brawls; or the way great armies of us are trained to fight,--not liking it much, and yet doing more killing in war-time and shedding more blood than even the fiercest lion on his cruelest days. Which would perplex a gentlemanly super-cat spectator the more, our habits of wholesale slaughter in the field, or our spiritless making a fetish of "order," at home?

It is fair to judge peoples by the rights they will sacrifice most for. Super-cat-men would have been outraged, had their right of personal combat been questioned. The simian submits with odd readiness to the loss of this privilege. What outrages him is to make him stop wagging his tongue. He becomes most excited and passionate about the right of free speech, even going so far in his emotion as to declare it is sacred.

He looks upon other creatures pityingly because they are dumb. If one of his own children is born dumb, he counts it a tragedy. Even that mere hesitation in speech, known as stammering, he deems a misfortune.

So precious to a simian is the privilege of making sounds with his tongue, that when he wishes to punish severely those men he calls criminals, he forbids them to chatter, and forces them by threats to be silent. It is felt that this punishment is entirely too cruel however, and that even the worst offenders should be allowed to talk part of each day.

Whatever a simian does, there must always be some talking about it. He can't even make peace without a kind of chatter called a peace conference. Super-cats would not have had to "make" peace: they would have just walked off and stopped fighting.

In a world of super-cat-men, I suppose there would have been fewer sailors; and people would have cared less for seaside resorts, or for swimming. Cats hate getting wet, so men descended from them might have hated it. They would have felt that even going in wading was a sign of great hardihood, and only the most daring young fellows, showing off, would have done it.

Among them there would have been no anti-vivisection societies:

No Young Cats Christian Associations or Red Cross work:

No vegetarians:

No early closing laws:

Much more hunting and trapping:

No riding to hounds; that's pure simian. Just think how it would have entranced the old-time monkeys to foresee such a game! A game where they'd all prance off on captured horses, tearing pell-mell through the woods in gay red coats, attended by yelping packs of servant-dogs. It is excellent sport--but how cats would scorn to hunt in that way!

They would not have knighted explorers--they would have all been explorers.

Imagine that you are strolling through a super-cat city at night. Over yonder is the business quarter, its evening shops blazing with jewels. The great stock-yards lie to the east where you hear those sad sounds: that low mooing as of innumerable herds, waiting slaughter. Beyond lie the silent aquariums and the crates of fresh mice. (They raise mice instead of hens in the country, in Super-cat Land.) To the west is a beautiful but weirdly bacchanalian park, with long groves of catnip, where young super-cats have their fling, and where a few crazed catnip addicts live on till they die, unable to break off their strangely undignified orgies. And here where you stand is the sumptuous residence district. Houses with spacious grounds everywhere: no densely-packed buildings. The streets have been swept up--or lapped up--until they are spotless. Not a scrap of paper is lying around anywhere: no rubbish, no dust. Few of the pavements are left bare, as ours are, and those few are polished: the rest have deep soft velvet carpets. No footfalls are heard.

Punctilious, haughty, inflammable

There are no lights in these streets, though these people are abroad much at night. All you see are stars overhead and the glowing eyes of cat ladies, of lithe silken ladies who pass you, or of stiff-whiskered men. Beware of those men and the gleam of their split-pupiled stare. They are haughty, punctilious, inflammable: self-absorbed too, however. They will probably not even notice you; but if they do, you are lost. They take offense in a flash, abhor strangers, despise hospitality, and would think nothing of killing you or me on their way home to dinner.

Follow one of them. Enter this house. Ah what splendor! No servants, though a few abject monkeys wait at the back-doors, and submissively run little errands. But of course they are never let inside: they would seem out of place. Gorgeous couches, rich colors, silken walls, an oriental magnificence. In here is the ballroom. But wait: what is this in the corner? A large triumphal statue--of a cat overcoming a dog. And look at this dining-room, its exquisite appointments, its daintiness: faucets for hot and cold milk in the pantry, and a gold bowl of cream.

Some one is entering. Hush! If I could but describe her! Languorous, slender and passionate. Sleepy eyes that see everything. An indolent purposeful step. An unimaginable grace. If you were *her* lover, my boy, you would learn how fierce love can be, how capricious and sudden, how hostile, how ecstatic, how violent!

Think what the state of the arts would have been in such cities.

They would have had few comedies on their stage; no farces. Cats care little for fun. In the circus, superlative acrobats. No clowns.

One of their poets

In drama and singing they would have surpassed us probably. Even in the stage of arrested development as mere animals, in which we see cats, they wail with a passionate intensity at night in our yards. Imagine how a Caruso descended from such beings would sing.

In literature they would not have begged for happy endings.

They would have been personally more self-assured than we, far freer of cheap imitativeness of each other in manners and art, and hence more original in art; more clearly aware of what they really desired, not cringingly watchful of what was expected of them; less widely observant perhaps, more deeply thoughtful.

Their artists would have produced less however, even though they felt more. A super-cat artist would have valued the pictures he drew for their effects on himself; he wouldn't have cared a rap whether anyone else saw them or not. He would not have bothered, usually, to give any form to his conceptions. Simply to have had the sensation would have for him been enough. But since simians love to be noticed, it does not content them to have a conception; they must wrestle with it until it takes a form in which others can see it. They doom the artistic impulse to toil with its nose to the grindstone, until their idea is expressed in a book or a statue. Are they right? I have doubts. The artistic impulse seems not to wish to produce finished work. It certainly deserts us half-way, after the idea is born; and if we go on, art is labor. With the cats, art is joy.

But the dominant characteristic of this fine race is cunning. And hence I think it would have been through their craftiness, chiefly, that they would have felt the impulse to study, and the wish to advance. Craft is a cat's delight: craft they never can have too much of. So it would have been from one triumph of cunning to another that they would have marched. That would have been the greatest driving force of their civilization.

This would have meant great progress in invention and science--or in some fields of science, the economic for instance. But it would have retarded them in others. Craft studies the world calculatingly, from without, instead of understandingly from within. Especially would it have cheapened the feline philosophies; for not simply how to know but how to circumvent the universe would have been their desire. Mankind's curiosity is disinterested; it seems purer by contrast. That is to say, made as we are, it seems purer to us. What we call disinterested, however, super-cats might call aimless. (Aimlessness is one of the regular simian traits.)

I don't mean to be prejudiced in favor of the simian side. Curiosity may be as debasing, I grant you, as craft. And craft might turn into artifices of a kind which would be noble and fine. Just as the ignorant and fitful curiosity of some little monkey is hardly to be compared to the astronomer's magnificent search, so the craft and cunning we see in our pussies would bear small relation to the high-minded planning of some ruler of the race we are imagining.

And yet--craft *is* self-defeating in the end. Transmute it into its finest possible form, let it be as subtle and civilized as you please, as yearning and noble, as enlightened, it still sets itself over against the wholeness of things; its rôle is that of the part at war with the whole. Milton's Lucifer had the mind of a fine super-cat.

That craft may defeat itself in the end, however, is not the real point. That doesn't explain why the lions aren't ruling the planet. The trouble is, it would defeat itself in the beginning. It would have too bitterly stressed the struggle for existence. Conflict and struggle make civilizations virile, but they do not by themselves make civilizations. Mutual aid and support are needed for that. There the felines are lacking. They do not co-operate well; they have small group-devotion. Their lordliness, their strong self-regard, and their coolness of heart, have somehow thwarted the chance of their racial progress.

SEVEN

There are many other beasts that one might once have thought had a chance.

Some, like horses and deer, were not bold enough; or were stupid, like buffaloes.

Some had over-trustful characters, like the seals; or exploitable characters, like cows, and chickens, and sheep. Such creatures sentence themselves to be captives, by their lack of ambition.

Dogs? They have more spirit. But they have lost their chance of kingship through worshipping us. The dog's finer qualities can't be praised too warmly; there is a purity about his devotion which makes mere men feel speechless: but with all love for dogs, one must grant they are vassals, not rulers. They are too parasitic--the one willing servant class of the world. And we have betrayed them by making under-simians of them. We have taught them some of our own ways of behaving, and frowned upon theirs. Loving us, they let us stop their developing in tune with their natures; and they've patiently tried ever since to adopt ways of ours. They have done it, too; but of course they can't get far: it's not their own road. Dogs have more love than integrity. They've been true to us, yes, but they haven't been true to themselves.

Pigs? The pig is remarkably intelligent and brave,--but he's gross; and grossness delays one's achievement, it takes so much time. The snake too, though wise, has a way of eating himself into stupors. If super-snake-men had had banquets they would have been too vast to describe. Each little snake family could have eaten a herd of cattle at Christmas.

Goats, then? Bears or turtles? Wolves, whales, crows? Each had brains and pride, and would have been glad to rule the world if they could; but each had their defects, and their weaknesses for such a position.

The elephant? Ah! Evolution has had its tragedies, hasn't it, as well as its triumphs; and well should the elephant know it. He had the best chance of all. Wiser even than the lion, or the wisest of apes, his wisdom furthermore was benign where theirs was sinister. Consider his dignity, his poise and skill. He was plastic, too. He had learned to eat many foods and endure many climates. Once, some say, this race explored the globe. Their bones are found everywhere, in South America even; so the elephants' Columbus may have found some road here before ours. They are cosmopolitans, these suave and well-bred beings. They have rich emotional natures, long memories, loyalty; they are steady and sure; and not narrow, not self-absorbed, for they seem interested in everything. What was it then, that put them out of the race?

Could it have been a quite natural belief that they had already won?

And when they saw that they hadn't, and that the monkey-men were getting ahead, were they too great-minded and decent to exterminate their puny rivals?

It may have been their tolerance and patience that betrayed them. They wait too long before they resent an imposition or insult. Just as ants are too energetic and cats too shrewd for their own highest good, so the elephants suffer from too much patience. Their exhibitions of it may seem superb,--such power and such restraint, combined, are noble,--but a quality carried to excess defeats itself. Kings who won't lift their scepters must yield in the end; and, the worst of it is, to upstarts who snatch at their crowns.

I fancy the elephants would have been gentler masters than we: more live-and-let-live in allowing other species to stay here. Our way is to kill good and bad, male and female and babies, till the few last survivors lie hidden away from our guns. All species must surrender unconditionally--those are our terms--and come and live in barns alongside us; or on us, as parasites. The creatures that want to live a life of their own, we call wild. If wild, then no matter how harmless we treat them as outlaws, and those of us who are specially well brought up shoot them for fun. Some might be our friends. We don't wish it. We keep them all terrorized. When one of us conquering monkey-men enters the woods, most animals that scent him slink away, or race off in a panic. It is not that we have planned this deliberately: but they know what we're like. Race by race they have been slaughtered. Soon all will be gone. We give neither freedom nor life-room to those we defeat.

If we had been as strong as the elephants, we might have been kinder. When great power comes naturally to people, it is used more urbanely. We use it as parvenus do, because that's what we are. The elephant, being born to it, is easy-going, confident, tolerant. He would have been a more humane king.

A race descended from elephants would have had to build on a large scale. Imagine a crowd of huge, wrinkled, slow-moving elephant-men getting into a vast elephant omnibus.

And would they have ever tried airships?

The elephant is stupid when it comes to learning how to use tools. So are all other species except our own. Isn't it strange? A tool, in the most primitive sense, is any object, lying around, that can obviously be used as an instrument for this or that purpose. Many creatures use objects as *materials*, as birds use twigs for nests. But the step that no animal takes is learning freely to use things as instruments. When an elephant plucks off a branch and swishes his flanks, and thus keeps away insects, he is using a tool. But he does it only by a vague and haphazard association of ideas. If he once became a conscious user of tools he would of course go much further.

We ourselves, who are so good at it now, were slow enough in beginning. Think of the long epochs that passed before it entered our heads.

And all that while the contest for leadership blindly went on, without any species making use of this obvious aid. The lesson to be learned was simple: the reward was the rule of a planet. Yet only one species, our own, has ever had that much brains.

It makes you wonder what other obvious lessons may still be unlearned.

It is not necessarily stupid however, to fail to use tools. To use tools involves using reason, instead of sticking to instinct. Now, sticking to instinct has its disadvantages, but so has using reason. Whichever faculty you use, the other atrophies, and partly deserts you. We are trying to use both. But we still don't know which has the more value.

A sudden vision comes to me of one of the first far-away ape-men who tried to use reason instead of instinct as a guide for his conduct. I imagine him, perched in his tree, torn between those two voices, wailing loudly at night by a river, in his puzzled distress.

My poor far-off brother!

The First Thinker

The First Thinker

EIGHT

We have been considering which species was on the whole most finely equipped to be rulers, and thereafter achieve a high civilization; but that wasn't the problem. The real problem was which would *do* it:--a different matter.

To do it there was need of a species that had at least these two qualities: some quenchless desire, to urge them on and on; and also adaptability of a thousand kinds to their environment.

The rhinoceros cares little for adaptability. He slogs through the world. But we! we are experts. Adaptability is what we depend on. We talk of our mastery of nature, which sounds very grand; but the fact is we respectfully adapt ourselves first, to her ways. "We attain no power over nature till we learn natural laws, and our lordship depends on the adroitness with which we learn and conform."

Adroitness however is merely an ability to win; back of it there must be some spur to make us use our adroitness. Why don't we all die or give up when we're sick of the world? Because the love of life is reënforced, in most energized beings, by some longing that pushes them forward, in defeat and in darkness. All creatures wish to live, and to perpetuate their species, of course; but those two wishes alone evidently do not carry any race far. In addition to these, a race, to be great, needs some hunger, some itch, to spur it up the hard path we lately have learned to call evolution. The love of toil in the ants, and of craft in cats, are examples (imaginary or not). What other such lust could exert great driving force?

With us is it curiosity? endless interest in one's environment?

Many animals have some curiosity, but "some" is not enough; and in but few is it one of the master passions. By a master passion, I mean a passion that is really your master: some appetite which habitually, day in, day out, makes its subjects forget fatigue or danger, and sacrifice their ease to its gratification. That is the kind of hold that curiosity has on the monkeys.

NINE

Imagine a prehistoric prophet observing these beings, and forecasting what kind of civilizations their descendants would build. Anyone could have foreseen certain parts of the simians' history: could have guessed that their curiosity would unlock for them, one by one, nature's doors, and--idly--bestow on them stray bits of valuable knowledge: could have pictured them spreading inquiringly all over the globe, stumbling on their inventions--and idly passing on and forgetting them.

To have to learn the same thing over and over again wastes the time of a race. But this is continually necessary, with simians, because of their disorder. "Disorder," a prophet would have sighed: "that is one of their handicaps; one that they will never get rid of, whatever it costs. Having so much curiosity makes a race scatter-brained.

"Yes," he would have dismally continued, "it will be a queer mixture: these simians will attain to vast stores of knowledge, in time, that is plain. But after spending centuries groping to discover some art, in after-centuries they will now and then find it's forgotten. How incredible it would seem on other planets to hear of lost arts.

"There is a strong streak of triviality in them, which you don't see in cats. They won't have fine enough characters to concentrate on the things of most weight. They will talk and think far more of trifles than of what is important. Even when they are reasonably civilized, this will be so. Great discoveries sometimes will fail to be heard of, because too much else is; and many will thus disappear, and these men will not know it."[1]

Let me interrupt this lament to say a word for myself and my ancestors. It is easy to blame us as undiscriminating, but we are at least full of zest. And it's well to be interested, eagerly and intensely, in so many things, because there is often no knowing which may turn out important. We don't go around being interested on purpose, hoping to profit by it, but a profit may come. And anyway it is generous of us not to be too self-absorbed. Other creatures go to the other extreme to an amazing extent. They are ridiculously oblivious to what is going on. The smallest ant in the garden will ignore the largest woman who visits it. She is a huge and most dangerous super-mammoth in relation to him, and her tread shakes the earth; but he has no time to be bothered, investigating such-like phenomena. He won't even get out of her way. He has his work to do, hang it.

Birds and squirrels have less of this glorious independence of spirit. They watch you closely--if you move around. But not if you keep still. In other words, they pay no more attention than they can help, even to mammoths.

We of course observe everything, or try to. We could spend our lives looking on. Consider our museums for instance: they are a sign of our breed. It makes us smile to see birds, like the magpie, with a mania for this collecting--but only monkeyish beings could reverence museums as we do, and pile such heterogeneous trifles and quantities in them. Old furniture, egg-shells, watches, bits of stone.... And next door, a "menagerie." Though our victory over all other animals is now aeons old, we still bring home captives and exhibit them caged in our cities. And when a species dies out--or is crowded (by us) off the planet--we even collect the bones of the vanquished and show them like trophies.

Curiosity is a valuable trait. It will make the simians learn many things. But the curiosity of a simian is as excessive as the toil of an ant. Each simian will wish to know more than his head can hold, let alone ever deal with; and those whose minds are active will wish to know everything going. It would stretch a god's skull to accomplish such an ambition, yet simians won't like to think it's beyond their powers. Even small tradesmen and clerks, no matter how thrifty, will be eager to buy costly encyclopedias, or books of all knowledge. Almost every simian family, even the dullest, will think it is due to themselves to keep all knowledge handy.

Their idea of a liberal education will therefore be a great hodge-podge; and he who narrows his field and digs deep will be viewed as an alien. If more than one man in a hundred should thus dare to concentrate, the ruinous effects of being a specialist will be sadly discussed. It may make a man exceptionally useful, they will have to admit; but still they will feel badly, and fear that civilization will suffer.

One of their curious educational ideas--but a natural one--will be shown in the efforts they will make to learn more than one "language." They will set their young to spending a decade or more of their lives in studying duplicate systems--whole systems--of chatter. Those who thus learn several different ways to say the same things, will command much respect, and those who learn many will be looked on with awe--by true simians. And persons without this accomplishment will be looked down on a little, and will actually feel quite apologetic about it themselves.

Consider how enormously complicated a complete language must be, with its long and arbitrary vocabulary, its intricate system of sounds; the many forms that single words may take, especially if they are verbs; the rules of grammar, the sentence structure, the idioms, slang and inflections. Heavens, what a genius for tongues these simians have![2] Where another race, after the most frightful discord and pains, might have slowly constructed *one* language before this earth grew cold, this race will create literally hundreds, each complete in itself, and many of them with quaint little systems of writing attached. And the owners of this linguistic gift are so humble about it, they will marvel at bees, for their hives, and at beavers' mere dams.

To return, however, to their fear of being too narrow, in going to the other extreme they will run to incredible lengths. Every civilized simian, every day of his life, in addition to whatever older facts he has picked up, will wish to know all the news of all the world. If he felt any true concern to know it, this would be rather fine of him: it would imply such a close solidarity on the part of this genus. (Such a close solidarity would seem crushing, to others; but that is another matter.) It won't be true concern, however, it will be merely a blind inherited instinct. He'll forget what he's read, the very next hour, or moment. Yet there he will faithfully sit, the ridiculous creature, reading of bombs in Spain or floods in Thibet, and especially insisting on all the news he can get of the kind our race loved when they scampered and fought in the forest, news that will stir his most primitive simian feelings,--wars, accidents, love affairs, and family quarrels.

To feed himself with this largely purposeless provender, he will pay thousands of simians to be reporters of such events day and night; and they will report them on such a voluminous scale as to smother or obscure more significant news altogether. Great printed sheets will be read by every one every day; and even the laziest of this lazy race will not think it labor to perform this toil. They won't like to eat in the morning without their papers, such slaves they will be to this droll greed for knowing. They won't even think it is droll, it is so in their blood.

Their swollen desire for investigating everything about them, including especially other people's affairs, will be quenchless. Few will feel that they really are "fully informed"; and all will give much of each day all their lives to the news.

Books too will be used to slake this unappeasable thirst. They will actually hold books in deep reverence. Books! Bottled chatter! things that some other simian has formerly said. They will dress them in costly bindings, keep them under glass, and take an affecting pride in the number they read. Libraries,--store-houses of books,--will dot their world. The destruction of one will be a crime against civilization. (Meaning, again, a simian civilization.) Well, it is an offense to be sure--a barbaric offense. But so is defacing forever a beautiful landscape; and they won't even notice that sometimes; they won't shudder anyway, the way they instinctively do at the loss of a "library."

All this is inevitable and natural, and they cannot help it. There even are ways one can justify excesses like this. If their hunger for books ever seems indiscriminate to them when they themselves stop to examine it, they will have their excuses. They will argue that some bits of knowledge they once had thought futile, had later on come in most handy, in unthought of ways. True enough! For their scientists. But not for their average men: they will simply be like obstinate housekeepers who clog up their homes, preserving odd boxes and wrappings, and stray lengths of string, to exult if but one is of some trifling use ere they die. It will be in this spirit that simians will cherish their books, and pile them up everywhere into great indiscriminate mounds; and these mounds will seem signs of culture and sagacity to them.

Those who know many facts will feel wise! They will despise those who don't. They will even believe, many of them, that knowledge is power. Unfortunate dupes of this saying will keep on reading, ambitiously, till they have stunned their native initiative, and made their thoughts weak; and will then wonder dazedly what in the world is the matter, and why the great power they were expecting to gain fails to appear. Again, if they ever forget what they read, they'll be worried. Those who *can* forget--those with fresh eyes who have swept from their minds such facts as the exact month and day that their children were born, or the numbers on houses, or the names (the mere meaningless labels) of the people they meet,--will be urged to go live in sanitariums or see memory doctors!

By nature their itch is rather for knowing, than for understanding or thinking. Some of them will learn to think, doubtless, and even to concentrate, but their eagerness to acquire those accomplishments will not be strong or insistent. Creatures whose mainspring is curiosity will enjoy the accumulating of facts, far more than the pausing at times to reflect on those facts. If they do not reflect on them, of course they'll be slow to find out about the ideas and relationships lying behind them; and they will be curious about those ideas; so you would suppose they'd reflect. But deep thinking is painful. It means they must channel the spready rivers of their attention. That cannot be done without discipline and drills for the mind; and they will abhor doing that; their minds will work better when they are left free to run off at tangents.

Compare them in this with other species. Each has its own kind of strength. To be compelled to be so quick-minded as the simians would be torture, to cows. Cows could dwell on one idea, week by week, without trying at all; but they'd all have brain-fever in an hour at a simian tea. A super-cow people would revel in long thoughtful books on abstruse philosophical subjects, and would sit up late reading them. Most of the ambitious simians who try it--out of pride--go to sleep. The typical simian brain is supremely distractable, and it's really too jumpy by nature to endure much reflection.

Therefore many more of them will be well-informed than sagacious.

This will result in their knowing most things far too soon, at too early a stage of civilization to use them aright. They will learn to make valuable explosives at a stage in their growth, when they will use them not only in industries, but for killing brave men. They will devise ways to mine coal efficiently, in enormous amounts, at a stage when they won't know enough to conserve it, and will waste their few stores. They will use up a lot of it in a simian habit[3] called travel. This will consist in queer little hurried runs over the globe, to see ten thousand things in the hope of thus filling their minds.

Their minds will be full enough. Their intelligence will be active and keen. It will have a constant tendency however to outstrip their wisdom. Their intelligence will enable them to build great industrial systems before they have the wisdom and goodness to run them aright. They will form greater political empires than they will have strength to guide. They will endlessly quarrel about which is the best scheme of government, without stopping to realize that learning to govern comes first. (The average simian will imagine he knows without learning.)

The natural result will be industrial and political wars. In a world of unmanageable structures, wild smashes must come.

TEN

Inventions will come so easily to simians (in comparison with all other creatures) and they will take such childish pleasure in monkeying around, making inventions, that their many devices will be more of a care than a comfort. In their homes a large part of their time will have to be spent keeping their numerous ingenuities in good working order--their elaborate bell-ringing arrangements, their locks and their clocks. In the field of science to be sure, this fertility in invention will lead to a long list of important and beautiful discoveries: telescopes and the calculus, radiographs, and the spectrum. Discoveries great enough, almost, to make angels of them. But here again their simian-ness will cheat them of half of their dues, for they will neglect great discoveries of the truest importance, and honor extravagantly those of less value and splendor if only they cater especially to simian traits.

To consider examples: A discovery that helps them to talk, just to talk, more and more, will be hailed by these beings as one of the highest of triumphs. Talking to each other over wires will come in this class. The lightning when harnessed and tamed will be made to trot round, conveying the most trivial cacklings all day and night.

Huge seas of talk of every sort and kind, in print, speech, and writing, will roll unceasingly over their civilized realms, involving an unbelievable waste in labor and time, and sapping the intelligence talk is supposed to upbuild. In a simian civilization, great halls will be erected for lectures, and great throngs will actually pay to go inside at night to hear some self-satisfied talk-maker chatter for hours. Almost any subject will do for a lecture, or talk; yet very few subjects will be counted important enough for the average man to do any *thinking* on them, off by himself.

In their futurist books they will dream of an even worse state, a more dreadful indulgence in communication than the one just described. This they'll hope to achieve by a system called mental telepathy. They will long to communicate wordlessly, mind impinging on mind, until all their minds are awash with messages every moment, and withdrawal from the stream is impossible anywhere on earth. This will foster the brotherhood of man. (Conglomerateness being their ideal.) Super-cats would have invented more barriers instead of more channels.

Discoveries in surgery and medicine will also be over-praised. The reason will be that the race will so need these discoveries. Unlike the great cats, simians tend to undervalue the body. Having less self-respect, less proper regard for their egos, they care less than the cats do for the casing of the ego,--the body. The more civilized they grow the more they will let their bodies deteriorate. They will let their shoulders stoop, their lungs shrink, and their stomachs grow fat. No other species will be quite so deformed and distorted. Athletics they will watch, yes, but on the whole sparingly practise. Their snuffy old scholars will even be proud to decry them. Where once the simians swung high through forests, or scampered like deer, their descendants will plod around farms, or mince along city streets, moving constrictedly, slowly, their litheness half gone.

They will think of Nature as "something to go out and look at." They will try to live wholly apart from her and forget they're her sons. Forget? They will even deny it, and declare themselves sons of God. In spite of her wonders they will regard Nature as somehow too humble to be the true parent of such prominent people as simians. They will lose all respect for the dignity of fair Mother Earth, and whisper to each other she is an evil and indecent old person. They will snatch at her gifts, pry irreverently into her mysteries, and ignore half the warnings they get from her about how to live.

Ailments of every kind will abound among such folk, inevitably, and they will resort to extraordinary expedients in their search for relief. Although squeamish as a race about inflicting much pain in cold blood, they will systematically infect other animals with their own rank diseases, or cut out other animals' organs, or kill and dissect them, hoping thus to learn how to offset their neglect of themselves. Conditions among them will be such that this will really be necessary. Few besides impractical sentimentalists will therefore oppose it. But the idea will be to gain health by legerdemain, by a trick, instead of by taking the trouble to live healthy lives.

Strange barrack-like buildings called hospitals will stand in their cities, where their trick-men, the surgeons, will slice them right open when ill; and thousands of zealous young pharmacists will mix little drugs, which thousands of wise-looking simians will firmly prescribe. Each generation will change its mind as to these drugs, and laugh at all former opinions; but each will use some of them, and each will feel assured that in this respect they know the last word.

And, in obstinate blindness, this people will wag their poor heads, and attribute their diseases not to simian-ness but to civilization.

The advantages that any man or race has, can sometimes be handicaps. Having hands, which so aids a race, for instance, can also be harmful. The simians will do so many things with their hands, it will be bad for their bodies. Instead of roaming far and wide over the country, getting vigorous exercise, they will use their hands to catch and tame horses, build carriages, motors, and then when they want a good outing they will "go for a ride," with their bodies slumped down, limp and sluggish, and losing their spring.

Then too their brains will do harm, and great harm, to their bodies. The brain will give them such an advantage over all other animals that they will insensibly be led to rely too much on it, to give it too free a rein, and to find the mirrors in it too fascinating. This organ, this outgrowth, this new part of them, will grow over-active, and its many fears and fancies will naturally injure the body. The interadjustment is delicate and intimate, the strain is continuous. When the brain fails to act with the body, or, worse, works against it, the body will sicken no matter what cures doctors try.

As in bodily self-respect, so in racial self-respect, they'll be wanting. They will have plenty of racial pride and prejudice, but that is not the same thing. That will make them angry when simians of one color mate with those of another. But a general deterioration in physique will cause much less excitement.

They will *talk* about improving the race--they will talk about everything--but they won't use their chances to *do* it. Whenever a new discovery makes life less hard, for example, these heedless beings will seldom preserve this advantage, or use their new wealth to take more time thereafter for thought, or to gain health and strength or do anything else to make the race better. Instead, they will use the new ease just to increase in numbers; and they will keep on at this until misery once more has checked them. Life will then be as hard as ever, naturally, and the chance will be gone.

They will have a proverb, "The poor ye have always with you,"--said by one who knew simians.

Their ingenious minds will have an answer to this. They will argue it is well that life should be Spartan and hard, because of the discipline and its strengthening effects on the character. But the good effects of this sort of discipline will be mixed with sad wreckage. And only creatures incapable of disciplining themselves could thus argue. It is an odd expedient to get yourself into trouble just for discipline's sake.

The fact is, however, the argument won't be sincere. When their nations grow so over-populous and their families so large it means misery, that will not be a sign of their having felt ready for discipline. It will be a sign of their not having practised it in their sexual lives.

ELEVEN

The simians are always being stirred by desire and passion. It constantly excites them, constantly runs through their minds. Wild or tame, primitive or cultured, this is a brand of the breed. Other species have times and seasons for sexual matters, but the simian-folk are thus preoccupied all the year round.

This super-abundance of desire is not necessarily good or bad, of itself. But to shape it for the best it will have to be studied--and faced. This they will not do. Some of them won't like to study it, deeming it bad--deeming it bad yet yielding constantly to it. Others will hesitate because they will deem it so sacred, or will secretly fear that study might show them it ought to be curbed.

Meantime, this part of their nature will be coloring all their activities. It will beautify their arts, and erotically confuse their religions. It will lend a little interest to even their dull social functions. It will keep alive degrading social evils in all their great towns. Through these latter evils, too, their politics will be corrupted; especially their best and most democratic attempts at self-government. Self-government works best among those who have learned to self-govern.

In the far distant ages that lie before us what will be the result of this constant preoccupation with desire? Will it kill us or save us? Will this trait and our insatiable curiosity interact on each other? That might further eugenics. That might give us a better chance to breed finely than all other species.

We already owe a great deal to passion: more than men ever realize. Wasn't it Darwin who once even risked the conjecture that the vocal organs themselves were developed for sexual purposes, the object being to call or charm one's mate. Hence--perhaps--only animals that were continuously concerned with their matings would be at all likely to form an elaborate language. And without an elaborate language, growth is apt to be slow.

If we owe this to passion, what follows? Does it mean, for example, that the more different mates that each simian once learned to charm, the more rapidly language, and with it civilization, advanced?

TWELVE

A doctor, who was making a study of monkeys, once told me that he was trying experiments that bore on the polygamy question. He had a young monkey named Jack who had mated with a female named Jill; and in another cage another newly-wedded pair, Arabella and Archer. Each pair seemed absorbed in each other, and devoted and happy. They even hugged each other at mealtime and exchanged bits of food.

After a time their transports grew less fiery, and their affections less fixed. Archer got a bit bored. He was decent about it, though, and when Arabella cuddled beside him he would more or less perfunctorily embrace her. But when he forgot, she grew cross.

The same thing occurred a little later in the Jack and Jill cage, only there it was Jill who became a little tired of Jack.

Soon each pair was quarreling. They usually made up, pretty soon, and started loving again. But it petered out; each time more quickly.

Archer felt bored

Meanwhile the two families had become interested in watching each other. When Jill had repulsed Jack, and he had moped about it awhile, he would begin staring at Arabella, over opposite, and trying to attract her attention. This got Jack in trouble all around. Arabella indignantly made faces at him and then turned her back; and as for Jill, she grew furious, and tore out his fur.

But in the next stage, they even stopped hating each other. Each pair grew indifferent.

Then the doctor put Jack in with Arabella, and Archer with Jill. Arabella promptly yielded to Jack. New devotion. More transports. Jill and Archer were shocked. Jill clung to the bars of her cage, quivering, and screaming remonstrance; and even blasé Archer chattered angrily at some of the scenes. Then the doctor hung curtains between the cages to shut out the view. Jill and Archer, left to each other, grew interested. They soon were inseparable.

The four monkeys, thus re-distributed, were now happy once more, and full of new liveliness and spirit. But before very long, each pair quarreled--and made up--and quarreled--and then grew indifferent, and had cynical thoughts about life.

At this point, the doctor put them back with their original mates.

And--they met with a rush! Gave cries of recognition and joy, like faithful souls reunited. And when they were tired, they affectionately curled up together; and hugged each other even at mealtime, and exchanged bits of food.

This was as far as the doctor had gotten, at the time that I met him; and as I have lost touch with him since, I don't know how things were afterward. His theory at the time was, that variety was good for fidelity.

"So many of us feel this way, it may be in the blood," he concluded. "Some creatures, such as wolves, are more serious; or perhaps more cold-blooded. Never mate but once. Well--we're not wolves. We can't make wolves our models. Of course we are not monkeys either, but at any rate they are our cousins. Perhaps wolves can be continent without any trouble at all, but it's harder for simians: it may affect their nervous systems injuriously. If we want to know how to behave, according to the way Nature made us, I say that with all due allowances we should study the monkeys."

To be sure, these particular monkeys were living in idleness. This corresponds to living in high social circles with us, where men do not have to work, and lack some of the common incentives to home-building. The experiment was not conclusive.

Still, even in low social circles--

THIRTEEN

Are we or are we not simians? It is no use for any man to try to think anything else out until he has decided first of all where he stands on that question. It is not only in love affairs: let us lay all that aside for the moment. It is in ethics, economics, art, education, philosophy, what-not. If we are fallen angels, we should go this road: if we are super-apes, that.

"Our problem is not to discover what we ought to do if we were different, but what we ought to do, being what we are. There is no end to the beings we can imagine different from ourselves; but they do not exist," and we cannot be sure they would be better than we if they did. For, when we imagine them, we must imagine their entire environment; they would have to be a part of some whole that does not now exist. And that new whole, that new reality, being merely a figment of our little minds, "would probably be inferior to the reality that is. For there is this to be said in favor of reality: that we have nothing to compare it with. Our fantasies are always incomplete, because they are fantasies. And reality is complete. We cannot compare their incompleteness with its completeness."[4]

Too many moralists begin with a dislike of reality: a dislike of men as they are. They are free to dislike them--but not at the same time to be moralists. Their feeling leads them to ignore the obligation which should rest on all teachers, "to discover the best that man can do, not to set impossibilities before him and tell him that if he does not perform them he is damned."

Man is moldable; very; and it is desirable that he should aspire. But he is apt to be hasty about accepting any and all general ideals without figuring out whether they are suitable for simian use.

One result of his habit of swallowing whole most of the ideals that occur to him, is that he has swallowed a number that strongly conflict. Any ideal whatever strains our digestions if it is hard to assimilate: but when two at once act on us in different ways, it is unbearable. In such a case, the poets will prefer the ideal that's idealest: the hard-headed instinctively choose the one adapted to simians.

Whenever this is argued, extremists spring up on each side. One extremist will say that being mere simians we cannot transcend much, and will seem to think that having limitations we should preserve them forever. The other will declare that we are not merely simians, never were just plain animals; or, if we were, souls were somehow smuggled in to us, since which time we have been different. We have all been perfect at heart since that date, equipped with beautiful spirits, which only a strange perverse obstinacy leads us to soil.

What this obstinacy is, is the problem that confronts theologians. They won't think of it as simian-ness; they call it original sin. They regard it as the voice of some devil, and say good men should not listen to it. The scientists say it isn't a devil, it is part of our nature, which should of course be civilized and guided, but should not be stamped out. (It might mutilate us dangerously to become under-simianized. Look at Mrs. Humphry Ward and George Washington. Worthy souls, but no flavor.)

In every field of thought then, two schools appear, that are divided on this: Must we forever be at heart high-grade simians? Or are we at heart something else?

For example, in education, we have in the main two great systems. One depends upon discipline. The other on exciting the interest. The teacher who does not recognize or allow for our simian nature, keeps little children at work for long periods at dull and dry tasks. Without some such discipline, he fears that his boys will lack strength. The other system believes they will learn more when their interest is roused; and when their minds, which are mobile by nature, are allowed to keep moving.

Or in politics: the best government for simians seems to be based on a parliament: a talk-room, where endless vague thoughts can be expressed. This is the natural child of those primeval sessions that gave pleasure to apes. It is neither an ideal nor a rational arrangement of course. Small executive committees would be better. But not if we are simians.

Or in industry: Why do factory workers produce more in eight hours a day than in ten? It is absurd. Super-sheep could not do it. But that is the way men are made. To preach to such beings about the dignity of labor is futile. The dignity of labor is not a simian conception at all. True simians hate to have to work steadily: they call it grind and confinement. They are always ready to pity the toilers who are condemned to this fate, and to congratulate those who escape it, or who can do something else. When they see some performer in spangles risk his life, at a circus, swinging around on trapezes, high up in the air, and when they are told he must do it daily, do they pity *him*? No! Super-elephants would say, and quite properly, "What a horrible life!" But it naturally seems stimulating to simians. Boys envy the fellow. On the other hand whenever we are told about factory life, we instinctively shudder to think of enduring such evils. We see some old workman, filling cans with a whirring machine; and we hear the humanitarians telling us, indignant and grieving, that he actually must stand in that nice, warm, dry room every day, safe from storms and wild beasts, and with nothing to do but fill cans; and at once we groan: "How deadly! What monotonous toil! Shorten his hours!"

His work would seem blissful to super-spiders,--but to us it's intolerable. The factory system is meant for other species than ours.

Our monkey-blood is also apparent in our judgments of crime. If a crime is committed on impulse, we partly forgive it. Why? Because, being simians, with a weakness for yielding to impulses, we like to excuse ourselves by feeling not accountable for them. Elephants would have probably taken an opposite stand. They aren't creatures of impulse, and would be shocked at crimes due to such causes; their fault is the opposite one of pondering too long over injuries, and becoming vindictive in the end, out of all due proportion. If a young super-elephant were to murder another on impulse, they would consider him a dangerous character and string him right up. But if he could prove that he had long thought of doing it, they would tend to forgive him. "Poor fellow, he brooded," they would say. "That's upsetting to any one."

As to modesty and decency, if we are simians we have done well, considering: but if we are something else--fallen angels--we have indeed fallen far. Not being modest by instinct we invent artificial ideals, which are doubtless well-meaning but are inherently of course second-rate, so that even at our best we smell prudish. And as for our worst, when we as we say let ourselves go, we dirty the life-force unspeakably, with chuckles and leers. But a race so indecent by nature as the simians are would naturally have a hard time behaving as though they were not: and the strain of pretending that their thoughts were all pretty and sweet, would naturally send them to smutty extremes for relief. The standards of purity we have adopted are far too strict--for simians.

FOURTEEN

We were speaking a while ago of the fertility with which simians breed. This is partly due to the constant love interest they take in each other, but it is also reënforced by their reliance on numbers. That reliance will be deep, since, to their numbers, they will owe much success. It will be thus that they will drive out other species, and garrison the globe. Such a race would naturally come to esteem fertility. It will seem profane not to.

As time goes on, however, the advantage of numbers will end; and in their higher stages, large numbers will be a great drawback. The resources of a planet are limited, at each stage of the arts. Also, there is only a limited space on a planet. Yet it will come hard to them to think of ever checking their increase. They will bring more young into existence than they can either keep well or feed. The earth will be covered with them everywhere, as far as eye can see. North and south, east and west, there will always be simians huddling. Their cities will be far more distressing than cities of vermin,--for vermin are healthy and calm and successful in life.

Ah, those masses of people--unintelligent, superstitious, uncivilized! What a dismal drain they will be on the race's strength! Not merely will they lessen its ultimate chance of achievement; their hardships will always distress and preoccupy minds,--fine, generous minds,--that might have done great things if free: that might have done something constructive at least, for their era, instead of being burned out attacking mere anodyne-problems.

Nature will do what it can to lessen the strain, providing an appropriate remedy for their bad behavior in plagues. Many epochs will pass before the simians will learn or dare to control them--for they won't think they can, any more than they dare control propagation. They will reverently call their propagation and plagues "acts of God." When they get tired of reverence and stop their plagues, it will be too soon. Their inventiveness will be--as usual--ahead of their wisdom; and they will unfortunately end the good effects of plagues (as a check) before they are advanced enough to keep down their numbers themselves.

Meanwhile, when, owing to the pressure of other desires, any group of primates does happen to become less prolific, they will feel ashamed, talk of race suicide, and call themselves decadent. And they will often be right: for though some regulation of the birth-rate is an obvious good, and its diminution often desirable in any planet's history, yet among simians it will be apt to come from second-rate motives. Greed, selfishness or fear-thoughts will be the incentives, the bribes. Contrivances, rather than continence, will be the method. How audacious, and how disconcerting to Nature, to baffle her thus! Even into her shrine they must thrust their bold paws to control her. Another race viewing them in the garlanded chambers of love, unpacking their singular devices, might think them grotesque: but the busy little simians will be blind to such quaint incongruities.

Still, there is a great gift that their excess of passion will bestow on this race: it will give them romance. It will teach them what little they ever will learn about love. Other animals have little romance: there is none in the rut: that seasonal madness that drives them to mate with perhaps the first comer. But the simians will attain to a fine discrimination in love, and this will be their path to the only spiritual heights they can reach. For, in love, their inmost selves will draw near, in the silence of truth; learning little by little what the deepest sincerity means, and what clean hearts and minds and what crystal-clear sight it demands. Such intercommunication of spirit with spirit is at the beginning of all true understanding. It is the beginning of silent cosmic wisdom: it may lead to knowing the ways of that power called God.

FIFTEEN

Not content with the whole of a planet and themselves too, to study, this race's children will also study the heavens. How few kinds of creatures would ever have felt that impulse, and yet how natural it will seem to these! How boundless and magnificent is the curiosity of these tiny beings, who sit and peer out at the night from their small whirling globe, considering deeply the huge cold seas of space, and learning with wonderful skill to measure the stars.

In studies so vast, however, they are tested to the core. In these great journeys the traveler must pay dear for his flaws. For it always is when you most finely are exerting your strength that every weakness you have most tells against you.

One weakness of the primates is the character of their self-consciousness. This useful faculty, that can probe so deep, has one naïve defect--it relies too readily on its own findings. It doesn't suspect enough its own unconfessed predilections. It assumes that it can be completely impartial--but isn't. To instance an obvious way in which it will betray them: beings that are intensely self-conscious and aware of their selves, will also instinctively feel that their universe is. What active principle animates the world, they will ask. A great blind force? It is possible. But they will recoil from admitting any such possibility. A self-aware purposeful force then? That is better! (More simian.) "A blind force can't have been the creator of all. It's unthinkable." Any theory *their* brains find "unthinkable" cannot be true.

(This is not to argue that it really is a blind force--or the opposite. It is merely an instance of how little impartial they are.)

A second typical weakness of this race will come from their fears. They are not either self-sufficing or gallant enough to travel great roads without cringing,--clear-eyed, unafraid. They are finely made, but not nobly made,--in that sense. They will therefore have a too urgent need of religion. Few primates have the courage to face--alone--the still inner mysteries: Infinity, Space and Time. They will think it too terrible, they will feel it would turn them to water, to live through unearthly moments of vision without creeds or beliefs. So they'll get beliefs first. Ah, poor creatures! The cart before the horse! Ah, the blasphemy (pitiful!) of their seeking high spiritual temples, with god-maps or bibles about them, made below in advance! Think of their entering into the presence of Truth, declaring so loudly and boldly they know her already, yet far from willing to stand or fall by her flames--to rise like a phoenix or die as an honorable cinder!--but creeping in, clad in their queer blindfolded beliefs, designed to shield them from her stern, bright tests! Think of Truth sadly--or merrily--eyeing such worms!

SIXTEEN

Imagine you are watching the Bandarlog at play in the forest. As you behold them and comprehend their natures, now hugely brave and boastful, now full of dread, the most weakly emotional of any intelligent species, ever trying to attract the notice of some greater animal, not happy indeed unless noticed,--is it not plain they are bound to invent things called gods? Don't think for the moment of whether there are gods or not; think of how sure these beings would be to invent them. (Not wait to find them.) Having small self-reliance they can not bear to face life alone. With no self-sufficingness, they must have the countenance of others. It is these pressing needs that will hurry the primates to build, out of each shred of truth they can possibly twist to their purpose, and out of imaginings that will impress them because they are vast, deity after deity to prop up their souls.

What a strange company they will be, these gods, in their day, each of them an old bearded simian up in the sky, who begins by fishing the universe out of a void, like a conjurer taking a rabbit out of a hat. (A hat which, if it resembled a void, wasn't there.) And after creating enormous suns and spheres, and filling the farthest heavens with vaster stars, one god will turn back and long for the smell of roast flesh, another will call desert tribes to "holy" wars, and a third will grieve about divorce or dancing.

All gods that any groups of simians ever conceive of, from the woodenest little idol in the forest to the mightiest Spirit, no matter how much they may differ, will have one trait in common: a readiness to drop any cosmic affair at short notice, focus their minds on the far-away pellet called Earth, and become immediately wholly concerned, aye, engrossed, with any individual worshipper's woes or desires,--a readiness to notice a fellow when he is going to bed. This will bring indescribable comfort to simian hearts; and a god that neglects this duty won't last very long, no matter how competent he may be in other respects.

But one must reciprocate. For the maker of the Cosmos, as they see him, wants noticing too; he is fond of the deference and attention that simians pay him, and naturally he will be angry if it is withheld;--or if he is not, it will be most magnanimous of him. Hence prayers and hymns. Hence queer vague attempts at communing with this noble kinsman.

To desire communion with gods is a lofty desire, but hard to attain through an ignobly definite creed. Dealing with the highest, most wordless states of being, the simians will attempt to conceive them in material form. They will have beliefs, for example, as to the furnishings and occupations in heaven. And why? Why, to help men to have religious conceptions without themselves being seers,--which in any true sense of "religious" is an impossible plan.

In their efforts to be concrete they will make their creeds amusingly simian. Consider the simian amorousness of Jupiter, and the brawls on Olympus. Again, in the old Jewish Bible, what tempts the first pair? The Tree of Knowledge, of course. It appealed to the curiosity of their nature, and who could control *that*!

And Satan in the Bible is distinctly a simian's devil. The snake, it is known, is the animal monkeys most dread. Hence when men give their devil a definite form they make him a snake. A race of super-chickens would have pictured their devil a hawk.

SEVENTEEN

What are the handicaps this race will have in building religions? The greatest is this: they have such small psychic powers. The over-activity of their minds will choke the birth of such powers, or dull them. The race will be less in touch with Nature, some day, than its dogs. It will substitute the compass for its once innate sense of direction. It will lose its gifts of natural intuition, premonition, and rest, by encouraging its use of the mind to be cheaply incessant.

This lack of psychic power will cheat them of insight and poise; for minds that are wandering and active, not receptive and still, can seldom or never be hushed to a warm inner peace.

One service these restless minds however will do: they eventually will see through the religions they themselves invented.

But ages will be thrown away in repeating this process.

A simian creed will not be very hard thus to pierce. When forming a religion, they will be in far too much haste, to wait to apply a strict test to their holy men's visions. Furthermore they will have so few visions, that any will awe them; so naturally they will accept any vision as valid. Then their rapid and fertile inventiveness will come into play, and spin the wildest creeds from each vision living dust ever dreamed.

They will next expect everybody to believe whatever a few men have seen, on the slippery ground that if you simply try believing it, you will then feel it's true. Such religions are vicarious; their prophets alone will see God, and the rest will be supposed to be introduced to him by the prophets. These "believers" will have no white insight at all of their own.

Now, a second-hand believer who is warmed at one remove--if at all--by the breath of the spirit, will want to have exact definitions in the beliefs he accepts. Not having had a vision to go by, he needs plain commandments. He will always try to crystallize creeds. And that, plainly, is fatal. For as time goes on, new and remoter aspects of truth are discovered, which can seldom or never be fitted into creeds that are changeless.

Over and over again, this will be the process: A spiritual personality will be born; see new truth; and be killed. His new truth not only will not fit into too rigid creeds, but whatever false finality is in them it must contradict. So, the seer will be killed.

His truth being mighty, however, it will kill the creeds too.

There will then be nothing left to believe in--except the dead seer.

For a few generations he may then be understandingly honored. But his priests will feel that is not enough: he must be honored uncritically: so uncritically that, whatever his message, it must be deemed the Whole Truth. Some of his message they themselves will have garbled; and it was not, at best, final; but still it will be made into a fixed creed and given his name. Truth will be given his name. All men who thereafter seek truth must find only his kind, else they won't be his "followers." (To be his co-seekers won't do.) Priests will always hate any new seers who seek further for truth. Their feeling will be that their seer found it, and thus ended all that. Just believe what he says. The job's over. No more truth need be sought.

It's a comforting thing to believe cosmic search nicely settled.

Thus the mold will be hardened. So new truths, when they come, can but break it. Then men will feel distraught and disillusioned, and civilizations will fall.

Thus each cycle will run. So long as men intertwine falsehoods with every seer's visions, both perish, and every civilization that is built on them must perish too.

EIGHTEEN

If men can ever learn to accept all their truths as not final, and if they can ever learn to build on something better than dogma, they may not be found saying, discouragedly, every once in so often, that every civilization carries in it the seeds of decay. It will carry such seeds with great certainty, though, when they're put there, by the very race, too, that will later deplore the results. Why shouldn't creeds totter when they are jerry-built creeds?

On stars where creeds come late in the life of a race; where they spring from the riper, not cruder, reactions of spirit; where they grow out of nobly developed psychic powers that have put their possessors in tune with cosmic music; and where no cheap hallucinations discredit their truths; they perhaps run a finer, more beautiful course than the simians', and open the eyes of the soul to far loftier visions.

NINETEEN

It has always been a serious matter for men when a civilization decayed. But it may at some future day prove far more serious still. Our hold on the planet is not absolute. Our descendants may lose it.

Germs may do them out of it. A chestnut fungus springs up, defies us, and kills all our chestnuts. The boll weevil very nearly baffles us. The fly seems unconquerable. Only a strong civilization, when such foes are about, can preserve us. And our present efforts to cope with such beings are fumbling and slow.

We haven't the habit of candidly facing this danger. We read our biological history but we don't take it in. We blandly assume we were always "intended" to rule, and that no other outcome could even be considered by Nature. This is one of the remnants of ignorance certain religions have left: but it's odd that men who don't believe in Easter should still believe this. For the facts are of course this is a hard and precarious world, where every mistake and infirmity must be paid for in full.

If mankind ever is swept aside as a failure however, what a brilliant and enterprising failure he at least will have been. I felt this with a kind of warm suddenness only today, as I finished these dreamings and drove through the gates of the park. I had been shutting my modern surroundings out of my thoughts, so completely, and living as it were in the wild world of ages ago, that when I let myself come back suddenly to the twentieth century, and stare at the park and the people, the change was tremendous. All around me were the well-dressed descendants of primitive animals, whizzing about in bright motors, past tall, soaring buildings. What gifted, energetic achievers they suddenly seemed!

I thought of a photograph I had once seen, of a ship being torpedoed. There it was, the huge, finely made structure, awash in the sea, with tiny black spots hanging on to its side--crew and passengers. The great ship, even while sinking, was so mighty, and those atoms so helpless. Yet, it was those tiny beings that had created that ship. They had planned it and built it and guided its bulk through the waves. They had also invented a torpedo that could rend it asunder.

It is possible that our race may be an accident, in a meaningless universe, living its brief life uncared-for, on this dark, cooling star: but even so--and all the more--what marvelous creatures we are! What fairy story, what tale from the Arabian Nights of the jinns, is a hundredth part as wonderful as this true fairy story of simians! It is so much more heartening, too, than the tales we invent. A universe capable of giving birth to many such accidents is--blind or not--a good world to live in, a promising universe.

And if there are no other such accidents, if we stand alone, if all the uncountable armies of planets are empty, or peopled by animals only, with no keys to thought, then we have done something so mighty, what may it not lead to! What powers may we not develop before the Sun dies! We once thought we lived on God's footstool: it may be a throne.

This is no world for pessimists. An amoeba on the beach, blind and helpless, a mere bit of pulp,--that amoeba has grandsons today who read Kant and play symphonies. Will those grandsons in turn have descendants who will sail through the void, discover the foci of forces, the means to control them, and learn how to marshal the planets and grapple with space? Would it after all be any more startling than our rise from the slime?

No sensible amoeba would have ever believed for a minute that any of his most remote children would build and run dynamos. Few sensible men of today stop to feel, in their hearts, that we live in the very same world where that miracle happened.

This world, and our racial adventure, are magical still.

TWENTY

Yet although for high-spirited marchers the march is sufficient, there still is that other way of looking at it that we dare not forget. Our adventure may satisfy *us*: does it satisfy Nature? She is letting us camp for awhile here among the wrecked graveyards of mightier dynasties, not one of which met her tests. Their bones are the message the epochs she murdered have left us: we have learned to decipher their sickening warning at last.

Yes, and even if we are permitted to have a long reign, and are not laid away with the failures, are we a success?

We need so much spiritual insight, and we have so little. Our airships may some day float over the hills of Arcturus, but how will that help us if we cannot find the soul of the world? Is that soul alive and loving? or cruel? or callous? or dead?

We have no sure vision. Hopes, guesses, beliefs--that is all.

There are sounds we are deaf to, there are strange sights invisible to us. There are whole realms of splendor, it may be, of which we are heedless; and which we are as blind to as ants to the call of the sea.

Life is enormously flexible--look at all that we've done to our dogs,--but we carry our hairy past with us wherever we go. The wise St. Bernards and the selfish toy lap-dogs are brothers, and some things are possible for them and others are not. So with us. There are definite limits to simian civilizations, due in part to some primitive traits that help keep us alive, and in part to the mere fact that every being has to be something, and when one is a simian one is not also everything else. Our main-springs are fixed, and our principal traits are deep-rooted. We cannot now re-live the ages whose imprint we bear.

We have but to look back on our past to have hope in our future: but--it will be only *our* future, not some other race's. We shall win our own triumphs, yet know that they would have been different, had we cared above all for creativeness, beauty, or love.

So we run about, busy and active, marooned on this star, always violently struggling, yet with no clearly seen goal before us. Men, animals, insects--what tribe of us asks any object, except to keep trying to satisfy its own master appetite? If the ants were earth's lords they would make no more use of their lordship than to learn and enjoy every possible method of toiling. Cats would spend their span of life, say, trying new kinds of guile. And we, who crave so much to know, crave so little but knowing. Some of us wish to know Nature most; those are the scientists. Others, the saints and philosophers, wish to know God. Both are alike in their hearts, yes, in spite of their quarrels. Both seek to assuage, to no end, the old simian thirst.

If we wanted to *be* Gods--but ah, can we grasp that ambition?

FOOTNOTES

[1] We did rescue Mendel's from the dust heap; but perhaps it was an exception.

[2] You remember what Kipling says in the Jungle Books, about how disgusted the quiet animals were with the Bandarlog, because they were eternally chattering, would never keep still. Well, this is the good side of it.

[3] Even in a wild state, the monkey is restless and does not live in lairs.

[4] From an anonymous article entitled "Tolstoy and Russia" in the *London Times*, Sept. 26, 1918.
